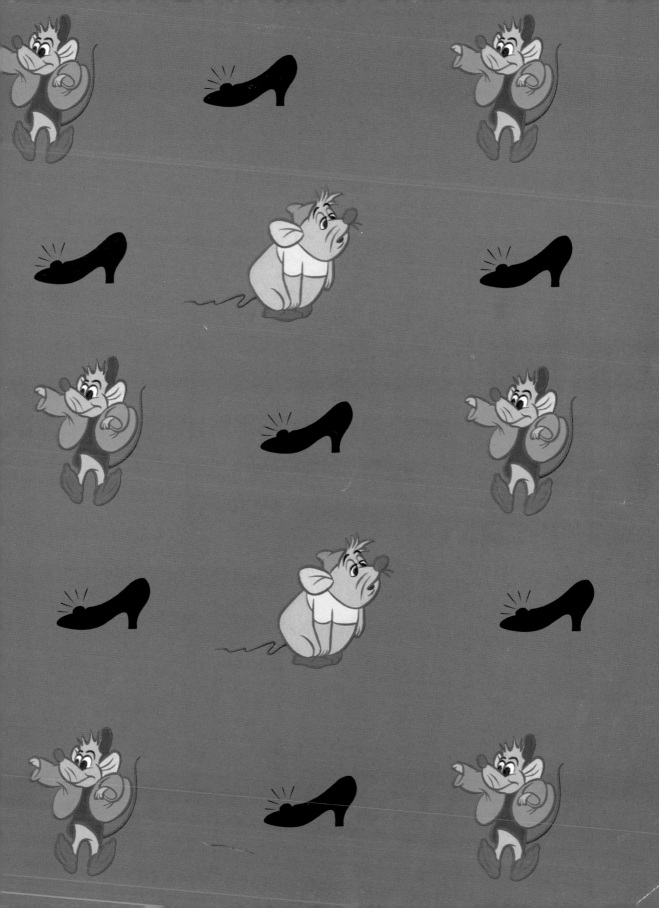

My First Disney Story

This is a book for you to share with your child time and time again.

Read the story aloud, pointing to the words as you go. Encourage your child to look at the pictures, and talk about the story and what she* can see. Ask questions about the action, and point out favourite characters. If your child is familiar with the story, she will enjoy telling you what is going to happen next! Encourage her to tell the story in her own words.

Above all, have fun sharing this favourite Disney tale with your child.

* To avoid the clumsy he/she and his/her we have referred to the child as she. All the books are, of course, equally suited to boys and girls, and all children will have their favourites.

A catalogue record for this book is available from the British Library

Published by Ladybird Books Ltd
A subsidiary of the Penguin Group
A Pearson Company
LADYBIRD and the device of a Ladybird are trademarks of Ladybird Books Ltd Loughborough Leicestershire UK
© Disney MCMXCVIII

DISNEY's
Cinderella

Ladybird

Cinderella lived in a castle with her stepmother and stepsisters. Her jealous stepmother made her live in the attic, and work as a servant. Cinderella's only friends were the birds and mice.

One morning Cinderella rescued a mouse from
a trap. She called him Gus and introduced him
to the other mice. Cinderella went outside to
feed the chickens. The mice went too, dodging
Lucifer the cat!

Suddenly an impatient voice shouted,
"Cinderella!"

It was time for Cinderella to take breakfast to her stepmother and stepsisters. She picked up their trays and carefully carried them upstairs.

Meanwhile, in the royal palace, the king was talking about his son.

"It's time the prince was married," he said to the grand duke. "I know – we'll give a ball this very night, and he can meet every maiden in the kingdom."

So the invitations went out straightaway.

When Cinderella's stepmother opened the royal invitation, she was very excited. "Every young girl is to go!" she said.

"May I go too, then?" asked Cinderella. Her stepsisters laughed cruelly. But her stepmother said, "Yes, if you do all your work first."

Cinderella was made to work all day, so she had
no time to get ready for the ball. But the mice
worked all day too, fixing a dress for her.

The dress had pretty ribbons, and Cinderella loved it. She put it on and hurried downstairs to go to the ball.

When Anastasia and Drizella saw how lovely Cinderella looked, they were jealous. They ripped her dress and ruined it. Then off they went to the ball in their carriage.

Cinderella went outside into the garden and cried and cried.

"Dry those tears," said a kind voice. It was her fairy godmother. "Now, we'll need a pumpkin," she said. Cinderella brought her one and the fairy godmother waved her wand.

The pumpkin turned into a coach! The mice
were turned into horses, the horse into a
coachman, and the dog into a footman!

The magic didn't stop. With another wave of the wand Cinderella was dressed in a beautiful ballgown with glass slippers on her little feet. "Off you go," said her fairy godmother. "But don't forget, on the last stroke of twelve, the spell will be broken…"

At the palace, Cinderella and the prince fell in love the moment they saw each other. Suddenly, the first stroke of midnight chimed...

Cinderella rushed out of the palace leaving one glass slipper behind her. By the last chime, she was dressed in rags. The spell was broken.

The prince was heartbroken at losing his true love. Next day, the grand duke was sent out to look for the girl whose foot fitted the glass slipper.

When he came to Cinderella's house her
stepmother had locked Cinderella in her room.
But Jaq and Gus found the key and set her free.

Cinderella hurried downstairs to try on the
slipper but it lay broken on the floor. She showed
the grand duke the other one. He was delighted
to have found her.

Soon afterwards, the prince and Cinderella were married. All Cinderella's friends went to the wedding… even the mice!